APR 1 5 2015

DATE DUE

FEB 2 4 2002
MAR 2 6 2010
APR 1 8 2016
AUG 1 1 2011
APR 1 0 2003
JAN 0 7 2004
SEP 2 6 2011
FEB 0 8 2004
OCT 2 4 2011
SEP 2 2 2005
MAR 2 2 2012
MAR 2 9 2014
JUL 1 0 2007
AUG 1 3 2012
SEP 1 7 2007
AUG 2 7 2012
SEP 2 3 2008
DEC 1 2 2008
AUG 1 0 2013
FEB 2 7 2010
MAY 2 3 2014
JAN 2 4 2015

Hans Christian Andersen

G. P. PUTNAM'S SONS
NEW YORK

Once upon a time there was an old widow who wished to have a child of her own. So she went to the wise woman of the village saying, "How I long for a little child. Can you help me?"

"Maybe I can, and maybe I cannot," replied the sage. "Take this magic barleycorn – it is not the kind that feeds the hens or grows in the fields – and plant it in a flowerpot. Then you shall see what you shall see."

"Thank you," said the widow, handing her a silver coin before hurrying home with the seed.

No sooner had she planted it than a tulip began to grow and bloom before her very eyes.

"What a pretty flower," she cried, kissing the petals. At once the tulip burst open with a pop. And in the very center of the flower sat a teeny tiny girl, neat and fair, and no bigger than the woman's thumb. So she called her Thumbelina.

CHILDREN'S ROOM

j398.2
ANDERSEN

The widow made a bed from a varnished walnut shell, a mattress out of violet leaves, and sheets from the petals of a rose. Here Thumbelina slept at night. In the daytime she played upon the table top. Sometimes she would row a little boat from one side of the lake to the other. Her boat was, in truth, a tulip leaf; her oars, two stiff white horsehairs; the lake, a bowl of water ringed with daisies. As she rowed, Thumbelina would raise her head and sing in a sweet, clear voice.

One night, however, while she lay sleeping in her cozy bed, a toad entered the room through a broken windowpane. It was big, wet and ugly, and it hopped upon the table where Thumbelina slept beneath her rose-petal sheet. When it saw the little child it croaked, "Here is the very wife for my son!"

Thereupon, it seized the walnut bed and hopped with it through the broken window and down into the garden.

Now, at the bottom of the garden flowed a stream; it was here, amid the mud and the slime, that the toad lived with her son. And that son was more loathsome than his mother.

"Croak, croak, cro-o-ak," was all he said when he saw the little maid.

"Hush, you'll wake her," said the mother. "We won't be able to catch her if she runs away; she's as light as dandelion fluff. I'll put her on a water-lily leaf and that way she'll be safe while we make your home ready for the wedding."

Out in the stream grew a host of water lilies, their broad green leaves floating on the water. The mother toad set Thumbelina down on the leaf farthest from the bank. When the poor girl awoke the next day she found herself stranded and began to cry. There was no way she could reach the safety of the bank.

Meanwhile, the old mother toad was busy deep down in the mud decorating the wedding home with bulrushes and buttercups. When she had finished, she and her ugly son swam together to the water lily.

"This is my son, your husband-to-be. You'll be nice and snug down in the mud with him," she croaked. Then off they swam.

Thumbelina wept. She did not want to live with the toads, nor to have the slimy son for a husband.

The little fishes in the water now popped up their heads to peer at the tiny maid. When they saw how sad she was, they decided to help her escape. Crowding about the leaf's green stalk, they nibbled on the stem until the leaf broke free. Slowly it drifted down the stream, bearing Thumbelina to safety.

On and on sailed the leaf, taking Thumbelina on a journey she knew not where.

For a time a dainty butterfly hovered overhead, then finally settled on the leaf. Thumbelina was so glad to have company that she took the ribbon from her waist and tied one end to the butterfly and one to the leaf. Now her boat fairly raced across the water, on and on and on. The radiant sun shone down upon the stream which glittered and glistened like liquid gold.

But Thumbelina's happiness was not to last. Presently, a large mayfly swooped down, seized her in its claws and flew up into a nearby tree. How frightened was poor Thumbelina as she soared through the air. Yet stronger than her fear was her sorrow for the butterfly; being still bound to the lily leaf it would be unable to feed itself and would surely die.

The mayfly, however, cared nothing for the butterfly. He set Thumbelina down upon the largest leaf, brought her honey from the flower pollen and sang her praises to the skies, even though she was nothing like a mayfly. By and by, all the mayflies that dwelt within the tree came to stare at the tiny girl. Two lady mayflies waggled their feelers in disgust, muttering scornfully, "But she has neither *wings* nor *feelers*. How ugly she is."

"Ugly, ugly, ugly," called all the mayflies in chorus.

The mayfly who had captured Thumbelina began to have his doubts; perhaps she really was as ugly as they said. Finally he made up his mind. He picked her up, carried her down to a daisy on the greenwood floor and left her there alone.

All through the summertime Thumbelina lived alone in the big, wide wood. She wove herself a gossamer bed and hung it beneath a broad dock leaf, to shelter her from the rain. She ate honey from the flowers and drank dew each morning from their leaves.

Summer and autumn passed, and cold winter began its long reign. The birds that sang so sweetly flew away and the trees and flowers shed their blooms. Her dock-leaf canopy withered to a yellow stalk.

Thumbelina began to tremble with the cold, for her clothes were now quite threadbare. She was so frail and slender, poor little mite, that she would surely freeze to death. Snow began to fall. Each fluffy flake that fell upon her head was like an avalanche.

Thumbelina wrapped herself in a withered leaf, but it gave her little warmth and she shook and shivered with cold.

Now, close by the wood lay a cornfield. The harvest had long been taken in, leaving dry stubble standing stiffly in the earth. To the tiny maid, the corn stalks were like a great forest. It was here that Thumbelina came in search of shelter. All of a sudden she stumbled upon a little house. It belonged to a fieldmouse who lived there, warm and snug and with a well-stocked larder. Like a little beggar girl, Thumbelina knocked timidly at the door. "Little mouse, little mouse, please let me in," she cried. "I've had nothing to eat for these past two days."

"You poor little thing," said the mouse. "Come into my warm house and dine with me."

The fieldmouse soon took a liking to the child. "Stay here through the winter," she said. "You can keep my home clean and tell me fairy stories; I do so love a good story."

One day the fieldmouse announced, "We're going to have a visitor; my neighbor is coming to tea. He is rather a splendid fellow, with a rich velvet coat and a house much grander than mine. He would make you a fine husband. His sight isn't good, poor thing, so you'll have to tell him your finest stories." The neighbor was a mole.

Thumbelina was not at all keen to wed a mole.

Next day the mole arrived, dressed in his fine black velvet coat. True, he was clever and learned, but he hated the light; he hated the sunshine and flowers, even though he had never seen them.

After tea, Thumbelina was called upon to read and to sing. She sang so beautifully that the mole fell in love with her at once. But this he kept to himself.

Mole had recently dug a tunnel from the fieldmouse's house to his own, so that they could visit each other when they liked. "Don't be afraid of the dead bird lying in the passage," he said. "It has no sign of injury and has all its feathers and its beak. Goodness knows how it got into my tunnel. It must have died of cold."

The mole took up a piece of rotten wood to use as a torch and led them down the tunnel. Then he pushed his long nose up through the soil to make room for daylight.

There lay a swallow, its wings pressed close by its sides, its head and legs drawn beneath it as if sheltering from the cold. The poor thing was frozen stiff.

Thumbelina felt so sad, for she loved the birds that had sung sweetly to her all through the summer. But the mole merely kicked the bird, saying, "Serves it right for all its chattering. How awful to be born a bird. I'm glad none of my children will be birds. All they do is chirrup the livelong day, then die of hunger once winter comes." The fieldmouse agreed.

Thumbelina was silent. Yet when the mole and the mouse had turned their backs, she bent down and kissed the swallow's eyes. Perhaps it was you who sang so sweetly to me, she thought.

That night Thumbelina could not sleep for thinking of the poor dead bird. At last she got up and wove a cover out of straw, carried it down the long dark passage and put it over the bird's still form. Then she fetched some blankets from the mouse's living room, putting them under the bird to protect it from the damp. "Farewell, pretty bird. And thank you for all your songs," she said. She pressed her head against the swallow's breast and was startled by a faint sound. The bird's heart was beating!

Thumbelina was now quite scared, for the bird was huge beside her. But she pressed the thistledown closer about its breast and fetched her own blanket to cover its head.

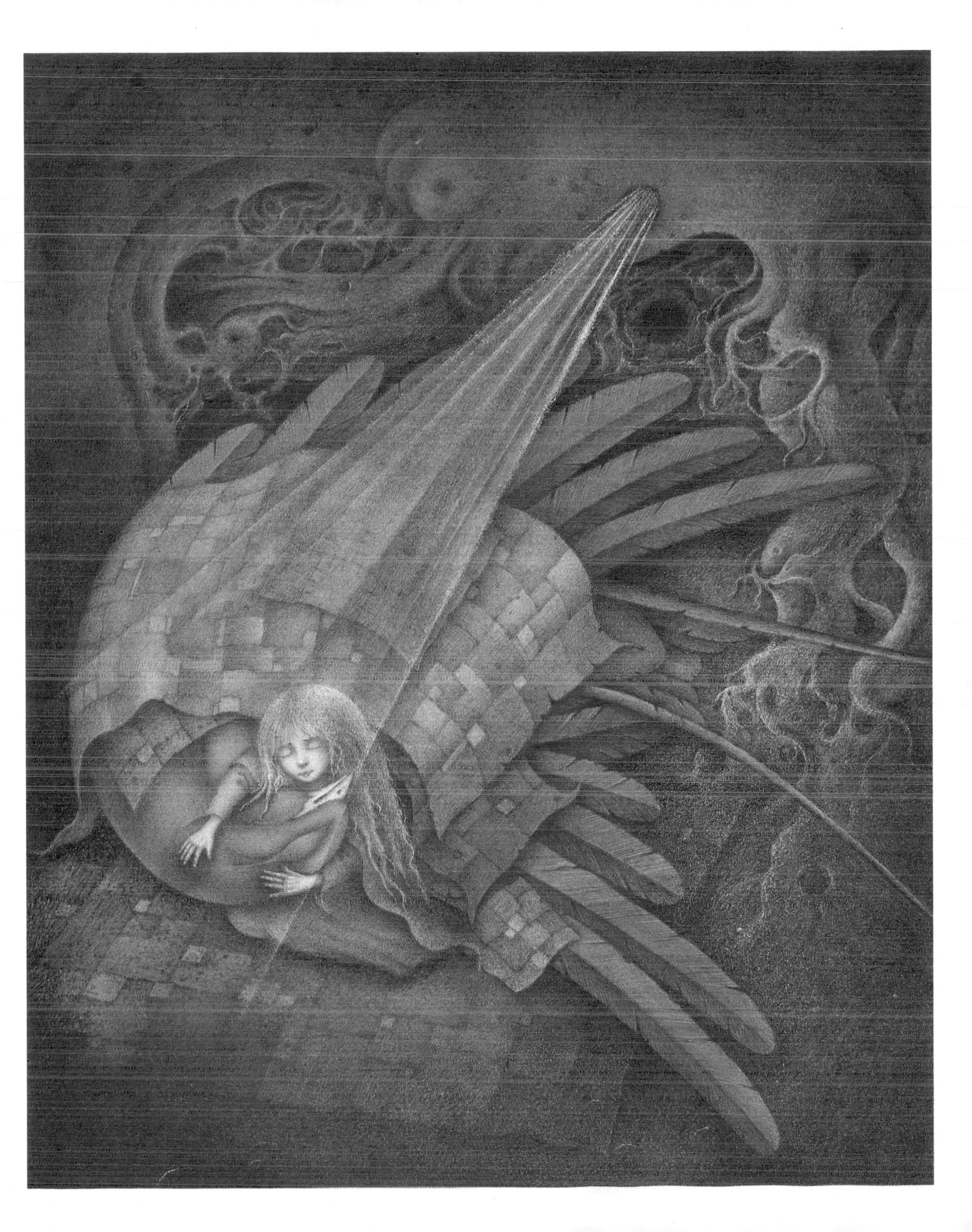

Next night she stole down the passageway again and was overjoyed to find the bird much better, although still weak.

"Thank you, little child," the swallow said. "Soon I'll be strong enough to fly out into the sunshine."

"Oh no," said Thumbelina, "you must stay here in your warm bed until you are strong. I will care for you."

The bird stayed underground the winter through, Thumbelina never breathing a word to the mole or mouse.

When spring arrived, it was time for the swallow to bid farewell. The tiny girl made a hole for it through the tunnel roof. How bright it was when the sun shone in.

"Come with me," said the swallow. "Sit upon my back and I'll take you far away to safety in the greenwood."

But Thumbelina thought the fieldmouse would be lonely without her, so she shook her head sighing, "I cannot."

"Farewell then, little Thumbelina," said the swallow as it soared into the spring sunshine. Sadly she watched him go.

Thumbelina was downcast. The corn would soon be so tall that the mouse's house would be hidden from the sun.

"You must spend your time preparing for your wedding," said the fieldmouse, for the mole had finally proposed. "You should sew your wedding dress, and make the linen for your household."

The mole hired four strong spiders to help spin the thread, and all through the summer Thumbelina spun and wove and sewed.

Every evening the mole came by to visit his wife-to-be, but all he said was, "Drat the summer. Hurry on winter." (For the sun baked the soil hard and made it difficult to dig. And once summer had passed and autumn came they would be wed.)

With every passing day Thumbelina began to dislike the mole more and more; he was so dull and vain. In the dusk of morning and in the evening sunset, she would tiptoe to the doorway and gaze out to catch a glimpse of the blue sky.

Autumn came and Thumbelina's wedding dress was ready. "Four weeks more and you'll be wed," said the fieldmouse.

Thumbelina wept. "I cannot marry the mole!" she cried.

"Nonsense!" said the mouse. "He'll make the perfect husband; his velvet coat is fit for a king; his house has many rooms and larders. You ought to think yourself lucky."

The wedding day arrived. Mole came to fetch his bride and take her to his deep-down house. She would never see the blue sky again, never feel the sun's rays, nor smell the flowers she loved. One last time she went outside to say goodbye to the world. She lifted up her arms toward the sky and stepped into the light. The corn was cut, but amid the stubble grew a lonely poppy bloom. "Farewell," she murmured. "If you see the swallow, give him my regards." Suddenly she heard a familiar sound.

"Tweet, tweet, tweet."

Looking up she saw her friend. Thumbelina told him all; how she had to marry the mole and live forever in the deep dark earth. She wept as she spoke.

"Winter will soon be here," said the swallow, "and I must fly away. Come with me; sit tight upon my back and we'll fly to a land where the sun always shines and where flowers blossom all the year through. You saved my life when I lay frozen and near death. Now it is my turn to help you."

Thumbelina climbed upon the swallow's back and up they soared, above forests and lakes and snowy mountains. She shivered in the frosty air and snuggled deep inside the bird's warm feathers.

At last they reached the land where the sun's breath was warm, the heavens blue and the clouds high. In the orchards, trees bent low with oranges and limes, and the scent of myrtle and lavender filled the air. But still the swallow did not stop. On it flew until it came to a tree-fringed lake. On the banks were the ruins of an ancient palace where many birds had built their nests among the creepers and clinging fronds.

"Choose a flower growing down below," said the swallow, "and there I will leave you to make your home." Thumbelina clapped her tiny hands.

On the soft green grass below lay fallen pillars of stone, around which grew pale, pure lillies. The swallow set her down upon a leaf. Imagine the girl's surprise when she saw a young man sitting in the center of the flower. He was just as tiny, just as neatly formed and dainty as herself; yet he was wearing a pair of wings. "How lovely he is," said Thumbelina to the swallow.

"In every flower there dwells a youth or maiden," said the bird. "Each one is the spirit of the flower."

The young man looked at Thumbelina and thought her the loveliest creature he had ever seen. Taking her hand, he asked her to be his bride. Now here was a better husband than the loathsome toad or the mole in the velvet coat. Thumbelina readily agreed.

Right at that moment there appeared from every flower a tiny boy or girl, each bearing a gift. But the best gift of all was a pair of wings to enable her to fly.

"You shall have a new name," said the flower spirit. "From now on we will call you Maya."

"Farewell then, Maya," sang the swallow as he took flight.

Soon he would start his journey north to Denmark. It was there he had a nest, above the window of a storyteller—Hans Christian Andersen by name—who wrote down the tale related here.

Text copyright © 1991 by James Riordan
Illustrations copyright © 1991 by Wayne Anderson

All rights reserved. This book, or parts thereof, may not be reproduced in any form without permission in writing from the publisher.
G. P. Putnam's Sons, a division of The Putnam & Grosset Book Group, 200 Madison Avenue, New York, NY 10016.
Originally published in Great Britain in 1990 by Hutchinson Children's Books, London
Printed and bound in Italy by L. E. G. O., Vicenza

Library of Congress Cataloging-in-Publication Data

Andersen, H. C. (Hans Christian), 1805–1875.
[Tommelise. English]
Thumbelina/Hans Christian Andersen.
p. cm.
Summary: A tiny girl no bigger than a thumb is stolen by a great ugly toad and subsequently has many adventures and makes many animal friends, before finding the perfect mate in a warm and beautiful southern land.

[1. Fairy tales.] I. Title
PZ8.A542Th 1990 90–7053 CIP AC
[E] — dc20
ISBN 0–399–21756–8

1 3 5 7 9 10 8 6 4 2

First impression

NOV 2001